MW01012985

for little artists — S.L.

Library of Congress Cataloging-in-Publication Data available.

ISBN 978-1-4521-5665-1

Manufactured in China.

Design by Sara Gillingham Studio.
Hand lettering by Suzy Lee. Typeset in Futura.
The illustrations in this book were rendered in pencil.

10 9 8 7 6 5 4 3 2 1

Chronicle Books LLC
680 Second Street
San Francisco, California 94107

Chronicle Books—we see things differently.
Become part of our community at www.chroniclekids.com.

lines

suzy lee

chronicle books · san francisco

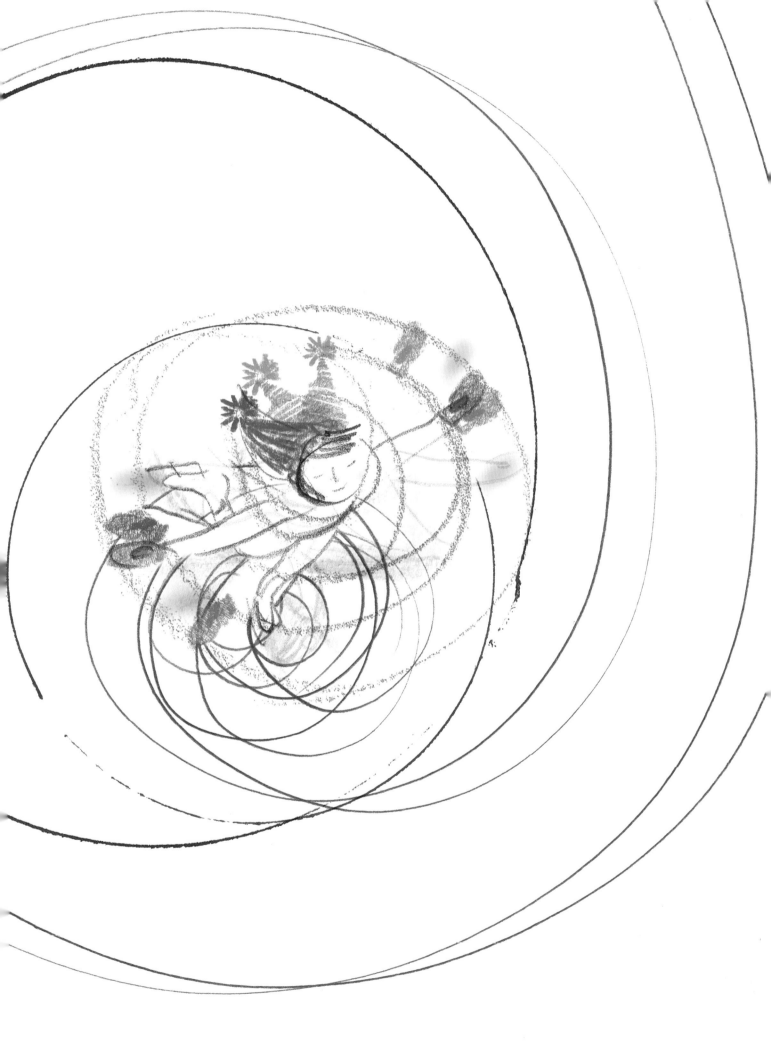